Henry's Big Mistake

LAUREN WHITMAN
Editor

JOE HOX
Illustrator

The Good News for Little Hearts series is written by Jocelyn Flenders. Jocelyn is a graduate of Lancaster Bible College with a background in intercultural studies and counseling. She is a writer and editor living in the Philadelphia area.

New Growth Press, Greensboro, NC 27401

Cover/Interior Illustrations: Joe Hox, joehox.com

ISBN: 978-1-64507-282-9

Library of Congress Cataloging-in-Publication Data
Names: Whitman, Lauren, author. | Hox, Joe, illustrator.
Title: Henry's big mistake : when you feel guilty / Lauren Whitman ; [illustrated by] Joe Hox.
Description: Greensboro : New Growth Press, 2022. | Series: Good news for little hearts | Includes index. | Audience: Ages 4-7. | Audience: Grades K-1. | Summary: After teasing his sister Halle, Henry Hedgehog develops a nagging feeling inside he cannot make go away, but when he learns about guilt and what God wants us to do after we sin, he gains the courage to make things right with God and Halle.
Identifiers: LCCN 2022005801 (print) | LCCN 2022005802 (ebook) | ISBN 9781645072829 (hardback) | ISBN 9781645072836 (ebook)
Subjects: CYAC: Guilt--Fiction. | Christian life--Fiction. | Brothers and sisters--Fiction. | Hedgehogs--Fiction. | Animals--Fiction. | LCGFT: Animal fiction. | Picture books.
Classification: LCC PZ7.1.W458 He 2022 (print) | LCC PZ7.1.W458 (ebook) | DDC [E]--dc23
LC record available at https://lccn.loc.gov/2022005801
LC ebook record available at https://lccn.loc.gov/2022005802

Printed in India

29 28 27 26 25 24 23 22   1 2 3 4 5

"So confess your sins to one another. Pray for one another so that you might be healed."

James 5:16a (NIrV)

On Friday afternoon,
Henry Hedgehog and his sister,
Halle, waved goodbye to
Miss Minnick and the
Mulberry Meadow School.

Fridays were their favorite days because they could play longer *and* later. And their mom made special snacks on Fridays—especially meant for sharing with friends.

Henry dashed across the field to find his best pals, Buster and Jax. Halle trailed behind with Freya and Delia.

As they all bounced through the meadow, the girls picked berries, nibbling as they went along.

Suddenly, Halle excitedly exclaimed, “I have a gweat idea! Let’s play the game where the animals eat pasghetti! We can make pasghetti out of gwass and the sauce out of mud!”

Ever since Halle had gotten braces, she had trouble saying certain words. Not all words—just some. Thankfully, her friends were kind about it. But it always got on Henry's nerves.

When he heard Halle misspeak,
Henry stopped in his tracks.

Halle exclaimed,
"Oh! Lellow daffodils! Let's gwab
them for our table!"

Henry rolled his eyes, "Good grief, Halle! You sound like a toddler! I can barely understand you! Grow up!"

Halle looked at Henry. She was squeezing the berries so tightly now that juice began streaming down her legs. Freya and Delia glared at Henry. Jax and Buster looked away nervously.

Henry laughed, "What?! Am I the only animal who can't understand her? Seriously?!"

Then he turned to his friends and said, "Come on! Let's race!"

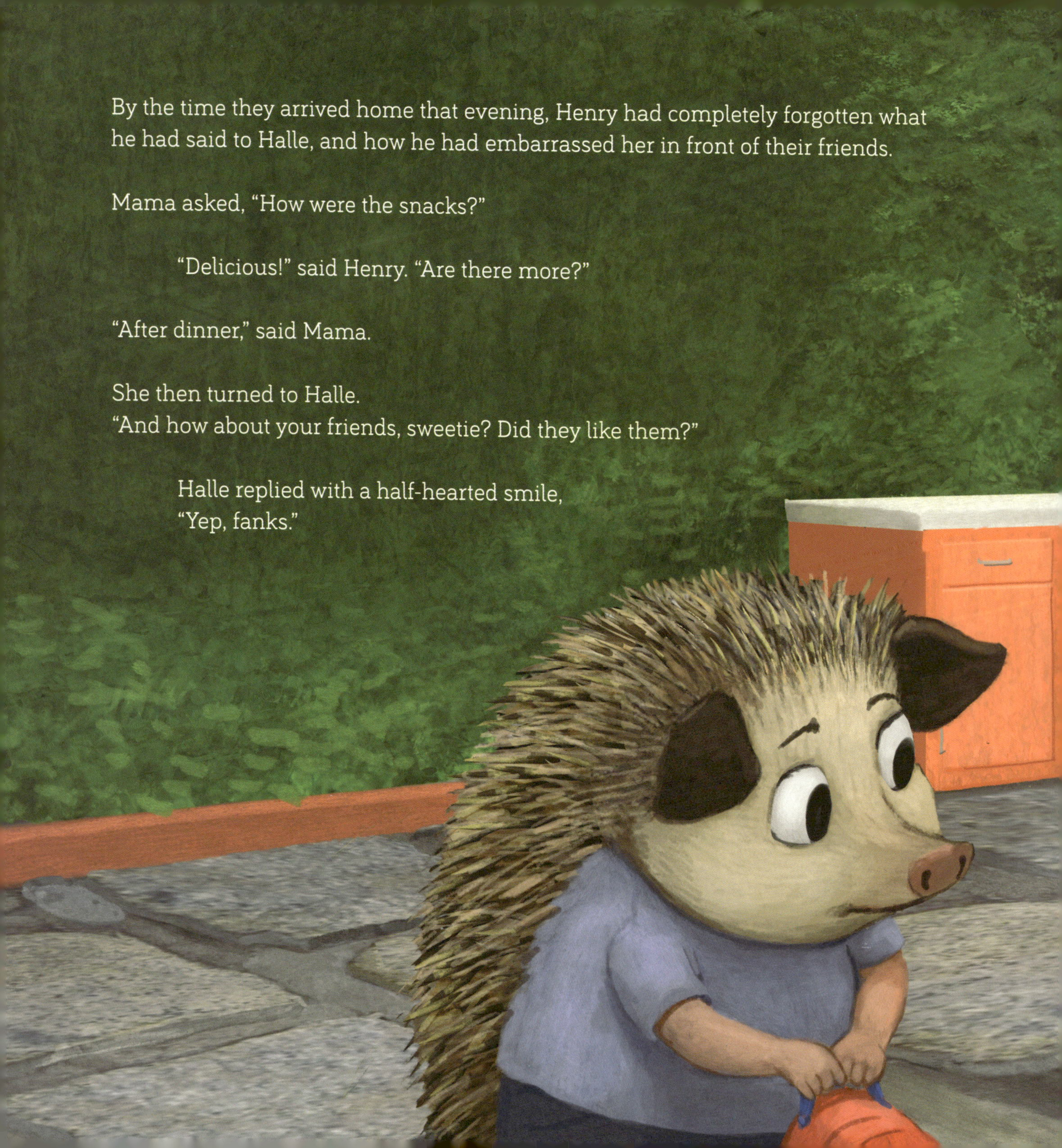

By the time they arrived home that evening, Henry had completely forgotten what he had said to Halle, and how he had embarrassed her in front of their friends.

Mama asked, “How were the snacks?”

“Delicious!” said Henry. “Are there more?”

“After dinner,” said Mama.

She then turned to Halle.
“And how about your friends, sweetie? Did they like them?”

Halle replied with a half-hearted smile,
“Yep, fanks.”

Halle usually had so much to say, but now she was quiet. She usually had stories to share, but now she just colored in silence.

What's going on with her? Henry wondered.

Now Henry *kind of* remembered their walk home. He *kind of* remembered Halle looking sad. But rather than think about it, he decided to just be extra nice to Halle. That would fix his mistake and smooth things over.

He complimented Halle's t-shirt.

He offered to play tag with her after dinner.

And to top it all off, he gave her the last maple-covered almond.

Henry thought, *Good, now we can move on from my mistake.*

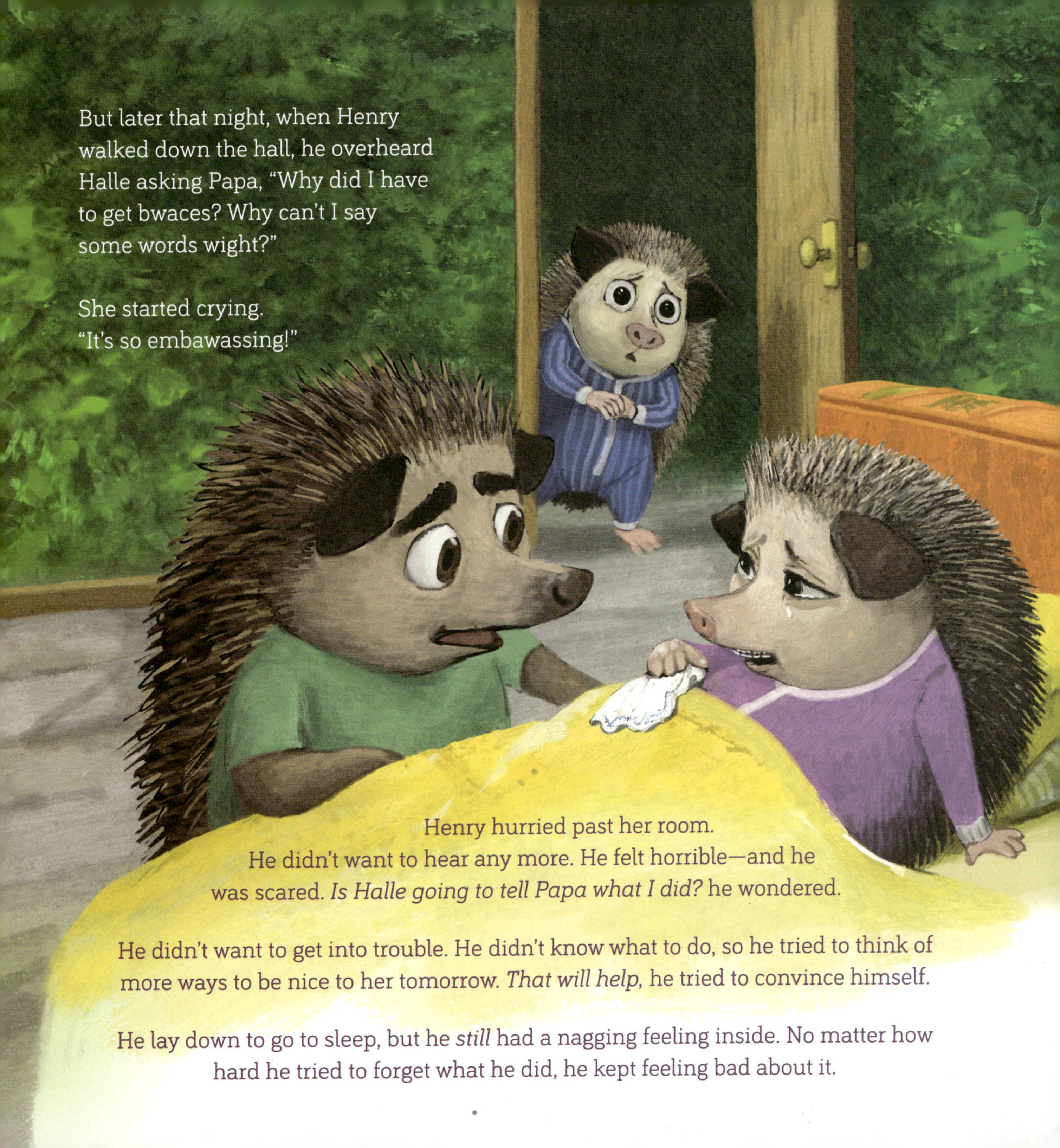

But later that night, when Henry walked down the hall, he overheard Halle asking Papa, "Why did I have to get bwaces? Why can't I say some words wight?"

She started crying.
"It's so embawassing!"

Henry hurried past her room.
He didn't want to hear any more. He felt horrible—and he was scared. *Is Halle going to tell Papa what I did?* he wondered.

He didn't want to get into trouble. He didn't know what to do, so he tried to think of more ways to be nice to her tomorrow. *That will help*, he tried to convince himself.

He lay down to go to sleep, but he *still* had a nagging feeling inside. No matter how hard he tried to forget what he did, he kept feeling bad about it.

On Sunday morning, the Hedgehog family set out for church. Halle still wasn't acting normally, especially around Henry. He missed playing with her. *At least she didn't tell on me*, Henry thought. He had been nervous all weekend waiting for Papa to talk to him, but he hadn't.

When they arrived at church, Henry and Halle joined their friends in Mrs. Bixby's Sunday school class. On the board, she wrote in big letters GUILT.

Just as Mrs. Bixby was about to begin the lesson, she was interrupted by a commotion. It sounded like a serious scuffle . . . between . . . ducks?

Mrs. Bixby set down her book. That's when Darcy Duck, Delia's older sister, came tumbling in.

Darcy shouted, "C'mon, Delia! Don't be mad. You look great!"

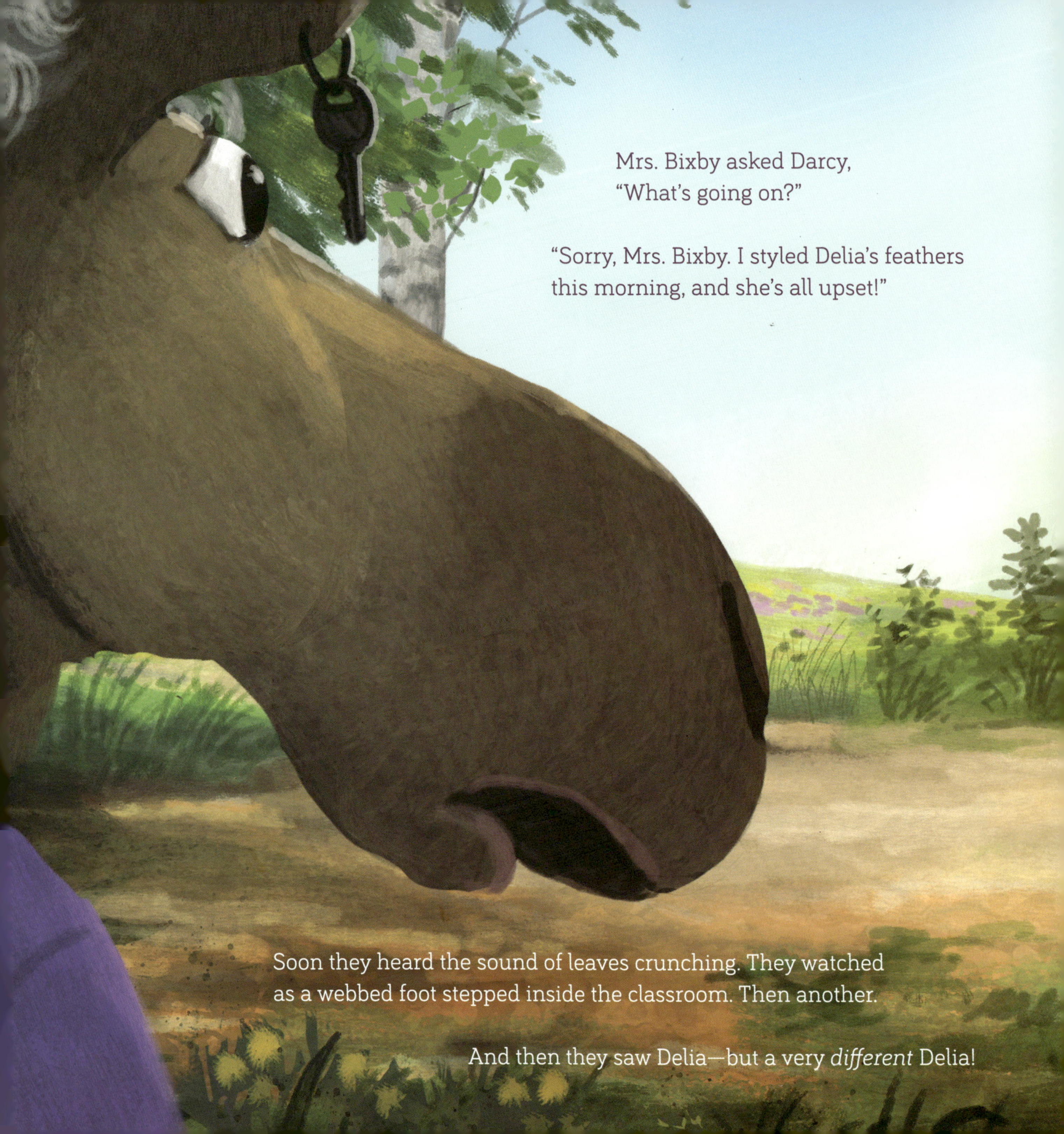

Mrs. Bixby asked Darcy,
"What's going on?"

"Sorry, Mrs. Bixby. I styled Delia's feathers this morning, and she's all upset!"

Soon they heard the sound of leaves crunching. They watched as a webbed foot stepped inside the classroom. Then another.

And then they saw Delia—but a very *different* Delia!

They saw a duck with the *biggest*, *craziest*, *wildest* tuft of feathers they'd ever seen! It looked like she'd just walked through a tornado! Her feathers were puffed out so high and so wide, they weren't even sure how she could walk!

Everyone gasped—even Mrs. Bixby. Darcy smirked as she watched Delia walk in. Clearly, Darcy had made Delia look silly on purpose.

Composing herself, Mrs. Bixby said,
"Oh, Delia, have a seat. We're so glad you're here!"

Delia chose a seat as far away from Darcy as she could get. She slunk down.

"Let's continue," said Mrs. Bixby. "It's well past time for our lesson. Speaking of *time*, how many of you use an alarm clock to wake up in the morning?"

Several hands went up.

"So do I!" said Mrs. Bixby. "Did you know that God has given us something similar to an alarm clock? If we do something wrong but haven't asked him for forgiveness, we feel bad. We call that bad feeling guilt."

"When we feel guilty, it's like that alarm buzzer is going off. It's time to do something! We need to go to God and ask for help. It's not time to hide our sin, or ignore it, or be quiet about it, but to come and tell God everything. That's called *confessing* our sins to God." She wrote CONFESS on the board next to GUILT.

Mrs. Bixby said, "The Great Book has a lot to say about this." She wrote, "People who conceal their sins will not prosper, but if they confess and turn from them, they will receive mercy." Proverbs 28:13

After they read the verse together, Mrs. Bixby said, "I once said something mean to my best friend, and I really hurt her feelings. I felt bad—really guilty—but I didn't tell God about my sin.

"When I saw my friend again, instead of asking for forgiveness, I acted like nothing had happened. Because I didn't confess my sin to God and ask for forgiveness, I kept feeling bad. I didn't feel happy; I felt guilty.

"That's what our verse means when it says we will not prosper. It wasn't until I asked God and my friend to forgive me that the guilt went away."

Suddenly, Henry saw things in a new light. He realized that all of his bad feelings that weekend were really his guilt! And he knew now why his attempts at making things better with Halle hadn't helped. He didn't just make a mistake; he had sinned. And he had tried to hide his sin and smooth it over without confessing it to God.

Mrs. Bixby passed out paper and said, "Let's write out today's verse so we can remember to always turn to God for help. Because Jesus died for our sins, God always forgives us when we come to him. And he gives us his Spirit who helps us to love others."

People who conceal their sins will not prosper, but if they confess and turn from them, they will receive mercy.

As Henry copied down the verse, he brought his guilt to God right then and there. He prayed silently,

Jesus, please forgive me for teasing Halle. I know it wasn't right and I'm so sorry that I hurt her feelings. Please help me not to do that again. And teach me how to really love her.

After he prayed, Henry decided he needed to talk to Halle the first chance he got so he could make things right with her the *right* way.

After church, Henry went and found Halle. “I was wrong to make fun of you, and to embarrass you. Will you forgive me?”

Halle’s eyes filled with tears. “You were so mean, Henwy!”

“I was,” he admitted. “And I’m sorry. When I first got braces, I had trouble saying some words too, but it got better. Yours will, too. I don’t want you to feel embarrassed about it. And I promise I won’t tease you again.”

“I don’t wemember that. You had twuble too?” Halle asked.

Henry nodded.

Halle smiled. “I do forgive you, Henwy.”

“Thank you, Halle!” He felt so happy and relieved.

On Monday morning, the Hedgehog home buzzed with excitement. Today Halle would receive a Science Star Award at school for her flipbook on cloud classifications!

At breakfast, Halle looked down at the dress that she had picked out for the special day. She said, "Don't you all just love my lellow dwess!"

Henry smiled at her and said,
"It's really nice. This award is a big deal, Halle! I'm so proud of you!"

Halle hugged Henry. "Fanks," she said, ". . . for *evwything*."

Before they left for school, the family prayed together to ask for God's blessing. Henry asked if he could pray for them.

"Please do, Henry. Thanks for offering," Papa said.

Henry prayed, "Dear God, thanks for this award and for how hard Halle worked on her project. Help us today to honor you in all we do. Help us to listen to your Spirit and turn to you for help. Bless us, we ask in Jesus's name,
Amen."

Henry and Halle bobbed across the meadow toward school. They met up with Buster, Jax, Freya, Darcy, and Delia.

Henry said to them, "Hey guys, I'm sorry for making you uncomfortable when I teased Halle on Friday. I was wrong, and Halle forgave me, thankfully."

"We're glad to hear all is well with the Hedgehog family!" Buster replied.

Darcy and Delia glanced at each other and smiled. It looked like all was well between them, too. And all was certainly well with Delia's feathers today!

"And there is more good news! Today Halle is getting an award!" Henry told them proudly.

Everyone congratulated Halle and she said, "Fanks, guys! Now who wants to wace to school?"

They all took off!

Helping Your Child with Feelings of Guilt

We can feel guilty for different reasons. Sometimes we feel guilty about accidents. For example, you're running the bases playing softball and collide with another player who falls and breaks their arm. Though you feel guilty and the person might be unhappy with you, you have not sinned. When children have accidents, a parent can explain how whatever it was that happened wasn't the child's fault (although it usually makes sense to apologize to the unhappy person). When we feel guilty about a non-moral matter such as the softball accident, this is false guilt.

This story is not about false feelings of guilt. It's about true guilt that comes after we sin. Remember that a child will probably need help understanding the word "sin." A short explanation is that sin is anything that is not loving toward God and people. Henry sinned against his sister by being unkind. He then *feels* guilty because he *is* guilty. His bad feelings are a clear sign of his need to confess his sin to God and ask his sister for forgiveness.

With an understanding of true guilt, teach your children what to do when they feel guilty. Here are some ideas:

1. **Help your child identify feelings of guilt.** Ask them how they feel after they've done something wrong. Feelings of guilt can be hard to describe, so put words to it for them. You can talk about how Henry felt throughout the weekend after he teased Halle. He worried his dad would find out. When he saw Halle was sad, he avoided her because he didn't know what to do. He tried to forget what happened—but he couldn't. He missed playing with her; their usual interactions changed because all wasn't right between them.

2. **Initiate conversations where you talk through instances of feeling guilty.** You go first. Similar to what Mrs. Bixby did for the children, offer an example from your life that can help them get a sense of guilt that comes after having sinned.

3. **In your home, create rhythms of both confession and seeking each other's forgiveness.** We sin every day, so make it normal and regular to confess sin and seek forgiveness from one another. Model this. Be on the lookout to do this; these are opportunities to lead by example, to model humility, and to show what it means to live in the light before God and others.

4. **Walk your children through the process of confession and restoration.** Model this process for them after *you* have sinned, and coach your child through these steps when *they* have sinned.

a. When we *confess* sin we put words to what we did that was wrong. We speak these words to God; we speak them to those we have hurt. We are specific.

b. After confessing sin, the next step is to ask God to *forgive* us for that specific wrong choice we made.

c. If we sinned against another person, we ask them to forgive us, too. Saying "I'm sorry," is not the same as saying "Please forgive me." Saying "Please forgive me" means you accept responsibility for sinning against the other person and that you recognize that you are in need of their mercy. Notice together with your child how Henry prayed to God for forgiveness and sought Halle's forgiveness. And, at the end of the book, he even acknowledges to their friends that his treatment of Halle in front of them put them in an uncomfortable situation.

d. Finally, we *give thanks* to God for forgiving us. In prayer, we thank God for his mercy. We thank him for removing the stain of sin from us. We thank him for Jesus who took the punishment for us so we could be recipients of God's grace.

5 **Talk to your children about how we can trust that God forgives us when we ask because this is what he promises to do in the Bible.** Trusting God means we believe that God forgives us—and we believe that he is even pleased to forget our bad choices! We trust that Jesus cleans us from all of our dirtiness. He will always meet us with his mercy when we come to him. He washes us as clean as clean can be, and then we are free to enjoy him and enjoy others, to serve him and to serve others (Hebrews 9:14)! There might be times we doubt that this could be true, and in those times we commit to rejecting the guilt and lean into God's gracious, reassuring words to us in verses like Isaiah 43:25 and 1 John 1:9. We speak about God's grace to one another, to our own hearts, and to God. He delights to show us mercy! He wants us to return to him and greets us joyfully when we do (Luke 15:11–32).

6 **Help your child see God's heart for them.** Life does not go well when we hide our sins (Proverbs 28:13)—and feeling guilty is one way life becomes difficult. But God wants our lives to go well! And we can be so sure of God's heart for us because he gave us Jesus, who took on the punishment of sin for us so we could be forgiven of our sins, and so we could be freed from the guilt that comes from our sin.

Notice together with your child how Henry felt after he made things right with God and Halle. Because God loves us, he wants us to be free of feeling guilty. The freedom and relief Henry felt is what God wants for us, too!

GOOD NEWS FOR LITTLE HEARTS

Back Pocket Bible Verses

Yes, what joy for those whose record the Lord has cleared of guilt, whose lives are lived in complete honesty!

Psalm 32:2

I confessed all my sins to you and stopped trying to hide my guilt. I said to myself, "I will confess my rebellion to the LORD." And you forgave me! All my guilt is gone.

Psalm 32:5

People who conceal their sins will not prosper, but if they confess and turn from them, they will receive mercy.

Proverbs 28:13

If we confess our sins, he is faithful and just and will forgive us our sins and purify us from all unrighteousness.

1 John 1:9 (NIV)

GOOD NEWS FOR LITTLE HEARTS

Back Pocket Bible Verses

WHEN YOU FEEL GUILTY

WHEN YOU FEEL GUILTY

GOOD NEWS FOR LITTLE HEARTS

GOOD NEWS FOR LITTLE HEARTS

WHEN YOU FEEL GUILTY

WHEN YOU FEEL GUILTY

GOOD NEWS FOR LITTLE HEARTS

GOOD NEWS FOR LITTLE HEARTS